HELP! MOM! HOLLYWOOD'S IN MY HAMPER!

Another Small Lesson in Conservatism

By Katharine DeBrecht

Illustrated by Jim Hummel

Praise for the first book in the "Help! Mom!" series

"Our hat is off to Katharine DeBrecht, the author of *Help! Mom! There are Liberals Under My Bed!*"
—**Rush Limbaugh**

"With the nation's libraries and classrooms filled with overtly liberal children's books...*Help! Mom! There are Liberals Under My Bed!* is the book conservative parents have been seeking."
—**National Review Book Service**

"Can't wait for the sequel." —**Philippe Reines, press secretary to Senator Hillary Rodham Clinton**

"A dandy Christmas present for young and inquiring minds."
—**Pittsburgh Tribune-Review**

"Brainwashing!" —**Alan Colmes, co-host "Hannity & Colmes"**
(coming from a liberal like Alan, we take that as a compliment)

For you,
Mom and Dad

Published by World Ahead Publishing, Inc., Los Angeles, CA

Copyright © 2006 by Katharine DeBrecht

World Ahead Publishing's books are available at special discounts for bulk purchases. World Ahead Publishing also publishes books in electronic formats. For more information, visit www.worldahead.com.

First Edition

ISBN 0-09767269-1-2
LCCN 2005939216
Printed in Mexico

Janie and Sam were sisters. And like most good girls, they did their chores, cleaned their room, remembered their manners, and giggled a lot, an awful lot!

And every day after they finished their homework, set the table, and fed their kitty, they watched their favorite TV show, *Stars Know Best*.

The girls loved watching all the glamorous stars on TV and often thought how fun it would be to dress and act like them.

But Janie and Sam had a problem. The clothes that the stars wore were very expensive, and the girls were already saving their money to buy new bikes.

Luckily, the girls had a plan. They were going to babysit to earn extra money, and their first job was that night.

"I'm so excited!" Janie told Sam.

"Me, too," Sam beamed, "and if we make enough money, we can buy the X400!"

The X400 was the coolest bike at Daniel's Bike Store on Main Street. The entire bike was hot pink and it even came with a hot pink walkie-talkie set so X400 riders could talk to each other.

The girls' very first job was to babysit for Ben and his little sister, Molly, who lived next door. Ben and Molly were a lot of fun. Ben liked to show the girls his slimy bug collection and Molly always squealed with delight when she saw Janie and Sam on the sidewalk.

In fact, there were plenty of nice kids in their small neighborhood for Janie and Sam to babysit. But the girls had already agreed they would never, EVER babysit for Billy down the street. He was wild—VERY WILD.

"I heard he dumped a bunch of worms in Riley Parker's purse," Janie squeaked.

"That was after he put scrambled eggs in her shoes!" Sam exclaimed.

The girls left for their job, and an hour and a half later, they returned home.

Janie plopped on her bed. "Whew! That was fun!"

"Yeah," Sam grinned, "except when little Molly got a pea stuck in her nose and when Ben found out that grasshoppers can't swim in the potty!"

The girls had tried to tell Ben that Gerald, his grasshopper, couldn't swim and that kids shouldn't play in the potty anyway, but Ben couldn't be convinced. When Gerald turned out not to be quite the swimmer Ben had hoped, Ben got pretty upset. However, after a quick funeral and a flush, Ben was off happily playing checkers with Norman, his caterpillar.

Thinking about Ben and Molly made the girls giggle as they got ready for bed.

Soon, they were giggling so much they actually thought their beds were shaking! But they weren't making the beds shake; it was a loud rumbling coming from behind their closet doors!

Before Sam could climb off her bed to grab the kitty, the closet doors burst open with a *WHOOSH* and a dozen flashes of bright light! The girls rushed over to the closet to find that it had transformed itself into a skybox with glass windows overlooking Hollywood.

The only thing left in the closet was a pink-checked hamper that their grandma had given them last Christmas. Camera lights flashed everywhere and cries of "Hurray for Hollywood" echoed in the background.

Surprised at the new state of their closet, Janie opened her mouth to say something to Sam, but before Janie could speak, the hamper began shaking and then—*BOING!*—a decked-out star popped out like a jack-in-the-box.

"Daisy Smears the Movie Star!" the girls screamed as the star bounced out of the hamper and then stumbled out of the closet. "What are *you* doing here?"

"Well," Daisy sighed as she eyed the girls with disapproval and popped a piece of Daisy Gum into her mouth, "it's clear that the first thing I'm gonna have to do is give you two a fashion lesson."

"Fashion lesson, ma'am?" Janie asked, remembering her manners.

"Oh, yes! Those clothes in your closet are *so* last year!" Daisy huffed, glancing at the girls. "Why, they're so out of style, they ♪♫*drive me craaaazy*♫♪" she crooned, breaking into song.

"But, ma'am, my mom says I always look nice." Janie blushed as she looked over at the pocket tee and jean skort she and her mom had bought on their special shopping trip two weeks ago.

"Parents!" Daisy scoffed. "What do *they* know about kids? What you *really* need is an official Daisy Flowerpot Hat," Daisy said, as she clumsily pulled a broken pot out of the hamper.

"Hey!" Sam cheered. "Mom stores broken pots in the garage! We can use those!"

"Oh no, no, no." Daisy shook her blonde curls adamantly. "You need the *official Daisy Flowerpot Hat—it's all the rage.*"

Daisy took out another pot and smacked it on her head with a *CRRAACK!* "There!" She admired herself in the girls' bedroom mirror. "That is *sooo* much better! Am I smart or what? Those socks must be working!"

"Did you say *socks*, ma'am?" Sam asked.

"Why, yes!" Daisy beamed. "Haven't you heard that if you wrap sweaty gym socks around your head, it makes you smarter?"

"What?" Janie looked puzzled.

"Oh, yes," Daisy replied. "I even opened a Daisy Smears Sock Institute to show kids how to use the power of socks to learn so they won't have to go to school!"

Daisy whipped out a bright blue sock from the hamper and wrapped it around her head. She pressed her index finger to her temple and began to think really hard. EUREKA! She brightened as though she had made a huge discovery and exclaimed loudly, "Milk comes from cows!"

"Um, ma'am?" Janie interrupted. "How much does the hat cost?"

"Well, let's see what you have." Daisy smacked her gum and pulled off the sock.

Sam showed Daisy their babysitting money.

"Is that *all?*" Daisy shuffled the money around in her hand. "Counting is *so* hard," she moaned, "but I guess this will have to do." Daisy stuffed the money into her Daisy Doorknob purse and twirled back into the closet.

"By the way," she cooed, poking her head out one last time, "that manners thing has got to go. It's *sooo uncool.* Buy tickets to my movie *Manners Are Mud,* and you'll see."

"But we don't have any money left to buy tickets," Sam whispered.

"Well, I should get going," Daisy said, sticking her gum behind her ear. "I am the special guest at the Boycott Velcro March." She handed the girls a flyer. "They need me because I am a STAR—which makes me an EXPERT on *everything.*"

And with that Daisy disappeared down the hamper, leaving the sound of one of her songs drifting up into the girl's room: "♪♫♩*Oh, Oh, Give me a siiiign—I don't know how to tell time!* ♫♪ "

Not a minute after Daisy vanished, the girls heard a loud *BANG!* followed by an *OUCH!* Cautiously, they peered into their closet, which still looked like Hollywood.

They could see Daisy down on the street, blindfolded by gym socks and bumping into a street sign. "*EEEK!* I think I have something stuck to my shoe!" she cried.

As their closet door began to close, the girls could see Daisy chattering away in the back seat of a taxi, leaving only a crooked street sign and a dangling gym sock behind.

"That was weird," Sam said as she opened the closet doors, only to find that everything in the closet was back to normal.

"Tell me about it," Janie agreed.

Still shaking their heads in disbelief, the girls pinky-swore not to tell anyone about the closet. No one would believe them anyway. Not even Julie around the corner whose big brother, Carl, had convinced her that pickles give you pimples.

The next day Mrs. Tersley from two doors down called asking the girls to babysit for her twin boys, Timmy and Tony.

Soon enough, the girls were off to babysit for the twins, wearing their officially licensed Daisy Flowerpot Hats. An hour or two later, they returned home.

"Wow," Janie told Sam, "those boys were a lot of fun, but this flowerpot hat is giving me a headache!" She pulled off the pot and set it on her nightstand.

"Yeah," Sam agreed. "It kept falling off when I was chasing Tony and trying to take off that boot he stuck on his head." She scratched their kitty behind the ears.

Tony had spent most of the afternoon jumping around and yelling "I'm Bootman!" while Timmy tried to figure out how fast Rocky Road ice cream would melt in the clothes dryer.

Once the girls put the ice cream and boots off-limits and made use of the kitchen utensil drawer, they had a wonderful time being rescued by Timmy the Whisk Man and his faithful sidekick, Tony the Turkey Baster.

Swapping stories about Timmy and Tony got the girls giggling again. Just like before, their closet doors flew open and a lanky star flipped out of the hamper and slid out of the closet.

"Oh my gosh, it's Rayonna the Pop-Singer!" the girls shrieked.

"Yes, it is I," Rayonna said as she looked down at the girls.

"What are *you* doing here?" Sam asked.

Rayonna eyed the girls haughtily. "The flower pot is good, but the rest is bad—it is *sooo last month*. You need style, you need grace! You need expensive makeup on your face! Come on, let's vogue!"

The girls looked at each other, unsure of what to do.

"Okay," Rayonna sighed, impatiently lugging a bag out of the hamper. "I can see that my work is cut out for me. Let's start with what you really need most of all—Rayonna Pants."

"Rayonna Pants?" Janie looked puzzled.

"Yes," Rayonna pulled a huge pair of pants out of her bag. "Everyone who's anyone is wearing them. *It's all the rage.*"

"They look like clown pants," Sam whispered. "I don't think we could wear those to church."

Rayonna glared at Sam. "Church? *Hello!!!* Who goes to church nowadays?" She flipped her freshly styled hair. "I'm into Toenailology. It is *absolutely fascinating!*"

"Toe what?" Janie asked.

"*Toe-nail-ology,*" Rayonna replied. "Don't you know that smelling your feet unlocks the secrets of the universe?" Her eyes grew wide. "In fact, now that my new CD is out, I'm changing my name to Toejamma."

"How much do the Rayonna Pants cost?" Janie asked.

"How much have you got?" Rayonna said, taking the money out of Janie's hand. "Is this is *all* you have? It's just *barely* enough. After all, we *are* living in a material world!"

"But lucky for you," the slinky star continued, "I'm having a special this week—every pair of pants comes with my new perfume, Ode to Onions."

"*Onion* perfume?" Sam crinkled her little nose. "That doesn't seem like a very nice scent."

"Please, it's OR-GAN-IC," Rayonna said, "and *everyone* wears it. By the way, what is that smell?" Rayonna looked around.

"Oh," answered Sam, "it's our mom's chicken casserole."

"And our favorite. Mmmm," Janie sniffed the air and fell onto her bed.

"Chicken casserole?" Rayonna growled. "Anyone who's anyone in Hollywood is a *saladtarian*. The only thing I eat is turnip salad."

"Turnip salad? Yuck!" Sam cringed.

"I love it, so everyone should love it," Rayonna snapped. "Now I have to run," she said, tossing the girls her turnip salad recipe. "I have a Save the Cauliflower Benefit Concert to give. They need me, you see, because I am a STAR and therefore an EXPERT." With that, she disappeared back into the hamper.

Almost immediately, the girls heard a strange wailing noise. As they peeked into their closet, they could see a distraught Rayonna throwing a tantrum on the sidewalk, yelling, "Do something!" Her helicopter had landed in the middle of the street, blowing recipes out of her hand and all over Hollywood.

The pilot scooped up Rayonna and plopped her into the helicopter. The last glimpse the girls caught before their closet door shut was of the star sniffing her toes as the helicopter rose into the sky, leaving behind a trail of turnip salad recipes and excited reporters.

A few days later, Mrs. Carson from across the street called to ask the girls to babysit for Katie and her little brother Jack. Janie and Sam had hoped it was Mrs. Terlsey or Ben and Molly's mom but neither had called the girls to babysit again and the girls couldn't understand why.

"I saw Hannah Quinn babysitting for the twins yesterday," Janie recalled.

"I think I heard something about onions giving Molly the sniffles," Sam added.

The girls didn't question their lack of babysitting jobs for long, though. They were just glad to get another chance to start saving for their X400 bikes. They had spent all of their money on Daisy and Rayonna clothes and did not want to have to babysit for wild Billy down the street.

Time flew babysitting for Katie and Jack, and the girls found themselves back at home almost before they knew it.

"Well, that went pretty well," Janie said as she put on her fuzzy slippers and hopped on the bed next to her kitty. "Except that these Rayonna Pants kept getting caught on Jack's highchair. I ripped them when I was trying to balance a sippie cup on my head so Jack would stop flinging his macaroni and cheese at the window."

"Yeah," Sam agreed. "Katie kept sniffing my perfume and asking if I liked to play in the garbage." She carefully picked up the onion perfume from her nightstand and set it on the window sill.

"Besides," Sam held her stomach, "that turnip salad we ate for lunch didn't fill me up. My stomach growled the whole time!"

Before Sam could go down the hall to ask their mom for a snack, their closet doors began rumbling louder than ever and burst open with dozens of flashing lights! A glitzy but aging star shot out of the hamper like a cannonball and landed in the middle of their room with a " *Ta-da!*"

The girls stood wide-eyed, not recognizing the swanky celebrity posing in the middle of the room.

"Who-o-o-o are you?" Janie meekly asked.

The aging star's large mouth dropped open as she put her hands on her sequined hips. "Funny girl. Do you mean YOU DON'T KNOW WHO I AM?!" she demanded.

Sam took a guess. "Ah, well, uhh, the lady in the toilet cleaner commercial?"

"NO! NO! NO!" The lady began waving her arms. "I HAPPEN TO BE THE GREATEST ENTERTAINER EV-ER! Music! Movies! I am even a personal friend of a FORMER PRES-I-DENT!" Exasperated, she looked at the girls.

The girls looked blankly at the star.

"BARBARA BUTTERSAND!!!" she stomped her foot which let out a loud *BLOOP!*

"What was *that?*" Sam asked, startled.

"Why, these are my Barbara Buttersand Butter Boots," the aging star said, admiring her footwear before putting a powder puff to her cheeks.

"Butter Boots?" Janie asked.

"Of course! *Everyone* is wearing them. *It's all the rage.*" As Ms. Buttersand sauntered around the bedroom, the crystal-studded boots let out a loud "*BLOOP! BLOOP!*" with every step.

"Yikes!" Sam jumped. "Are you sure they don't scare people? My dad says it isn't nice to scare people like that."

"Excuse me?" Ms. Buttersand rolled her eyes. "What do *parents* know about what is nice or proper?! You should listen to me instead—after all, I received this year's Ms. Motormouth Award." She took a bow.

"Ms. Motormouth Award?" Sam asked.

"Oh, yes! Only the most *important* people receive the award, for telling everyone else what to do," said the star. "It's all for the *little people*—people who need Barbara!" She twirled. "In fact, that's why I sponsored National Ear Wax Day!"

Ms. Buttersand pulled out a cotton swab and sauntered over to the girls' mirror. She glanced at her reflection and exclaimed, "Hello, Gorgeous!"

The aging star spent the next two hours in front of the mirror, cleaning her ears and lecturing the girls on everything from having her picture put on a three-dollar bill to teaching *Babakaluka* instead of English in schools.

"How much do the Butter Boots cost?" Janie asked, interrupting the star's speech about Paperclip Safety Week.

"Well, let's see what you have." She snatched the babysitting money from Janie. *"This is it?"* Ms. Buttersand sighed and stuffed the money in her handbag, "It's not quite enough, but I'll come back for the rest later. And when I do, you can also pay for my signature radish earrings."

"Radish earrings?" Sam winced. "I don't even like to *eat* radishes."

"Everyone on TV wears them," Ms. Buttersand replied, glancing at her diamond watch. "I've got to go. I am hosting a dinner for Congresswoman Clunkton." She fluffed her hair one last time in the mirror. "Your parents *must* vote for her, by the way."

"I think they said they were voting for Mr. Valueson," Janie remembered.

"Mr. Valueson?" Ms. Buttersand shook her head, "All *he* talks about is family values and morals, as if *that* is important to people."

"I think it's kind of important," Janie whispered.

"Well," the aging star snapped, "Congresswoman Clunkton is the person for the job. I should know. I am a STAR and therefore an EXPERT. I am even a friend of a FORMER PRES-I-DENT," she crowed. "You see, Congresswoman Clunkton and I know what is best for all you *little people* in this world. She even passed a law to protect kids' teeth by banning sugar in lemonade! But my limo is waiting." She stuffed a fistful of ballots in the girls' hands. "I have to go."

Ms. Buttersand disappeared into the hamper. Within a few seconds the girls heard someone screaming and dashed over to the closet. They saw Ms. Buttersand on a Hollywood sidewalk, yelling and throwing ballots at her limousine driver. "A PARKING TICKET?! Get Congresswoman Clunkton on the phone NOW!" She marched up and down the sidewalk.

The girls couldn't hear anything else that Ms. Buttersand shouted—her Butter Boots kept spouting out *BLOOP! BLOOP! BLOOP! BLOOOOOOP!*

The girls watched as the closet doors closed and the limousine sped away with Ms. Buttersand hollering into her phone and leaving a trail of ballots and parking tickets behind.

The only babysitting call the girls had the next week was for wild Billy down the street and his cousin, Louise. The girls still didn't want to babysit for Billy, but decided they needed the money for the X400 and thought he wouldn't be as wild as usual since his cousin was visiting.

It did not go well.

Billy kept swatting at the girls' radish earrings and yelling "*Score!*" each time he hit one. Meanwhile, Louise screamed at every *BLOOP!* of the Butter Boots.

The girls finally decided to go barefoot so the boots wouldn't scare Louise and she eventually fell asleep. They also felt it was best to keep Billy occupied and out of trouble. They learned that Billy was an excellent Go Fish player. He beat the girls 23 games to 2!

When the girls got home, they flipped on *Stars Know Best*. Daisy Smears, Rayonna, and Barbara Buttersand were holding a press conference with Congresswoman Clunkton. Reporters were rushing up to the congresswoman to get soundbites and autographs. The politician chuckled and put her arms around the stars.

"These people are the heart and soul of America." The congresswoman grinned as she posed for a quick photo with the stars. "They're famous celebrities, so what they say and do is *very important*."

Rayonna added, "Even though we stars live very different lives from the *little people* in this world, we know what is best for them."

"We especially know how to spend the *little people's* money for them," Ms. Buttersand smirked. "If you're not on TV or in the movies, you need smart people in the government to tell you what to do..."

Ms. Buttersand's speech was interrupted by a loud POP! Everyone immediately turned toward Daisy, whose face was covered in bright pink Daisy Gum. "Oops, I did it again!" she giggled, and began peeling gum off her forehead.

Janie and Sam shook their heads as they turned off the TV and went to bed.

The next week the girls didn't get *any* calls to babysit—not even for wild Billy.

"I thought we were good with the kids," Janie said sadly.

Not a minute after Janie spoke, the girls heard another loud noise, but this time it came from outside. The girls ran over to their bedroom window. Hannah Quinn was on her new X400 bike, laughing aloud with her friends and wearing her pocket tee and jean skort like always. Hannah seemed to be babysitting a lot these days!

"Maybe it wasn't that great an idea to do all those things the stars told us to do." Janie pulled Sam in front of their mirror.

"Yeah," Sam agreed, looking at their reflection. "We *do* look kind of funny! Maybe that's why mom and dad always tell us that it's more important to be ourselves than to be like the stars on TV."

"Just because they're famous doesn't mean we have to do all the strange things they do—or spend all of our money trying to look like them." Janie pulled off her flowerpot hat.

"Come on," Sam playfully pushed Janie away from the mirror. "Let's change into our REAL clothes and go play with Hannah and the other kids!"

"Great idea," Janie said. "I think we are EXPERTS at being ourselves!"

The girls giggled as they changed into their regular clothes and ran outside to play with Hannah and their other friends. Piled in the garbage behind them they left all their star junk...*and it was all the rage.*

SPECIAL THANKS to my family and friends, especially my parents and siblings—including my Web King, Tom, for their continued support and enthusiasm; and, of course, my husband and children for being so much a part of this book in so many ways.

THANKS ALSO to all those Hollywood types whose antics make me laugh, at times make me cringe, but in all made writing this book so much fun. I am proud to say that none of the proceeds from this book will go to their ticket sales.

About the Author: Katharine DeBrecht is a mother of three. A freelance newspaper reporter who graduated cum laude from Saint Mary's College in Notre Dame, she served as South Carolina's co-captain of "Security Moms for Bush."

About the Illustrator: Jim Hummel is a professional illustrator and instructor at San Jose State University. A military veteran and former art director for the Associated Press, he is a past winner of the prestigious Reuben Award from the National Cartoonists Society.

Cast of Characters

The strange stars are gone for now, but they'll soon be back with
more flowerpots, more turnips, and even more Toenailology!

Be on the lookout for future "Help! Mom!" adventures in stores soon, and visit
our Web site at www.helpmombooks.com for special bonus material. If you would like
to receive periodic "Help! Mom!" related updates, email us at
helpmom@worldahead.com.

In the meantime, enjoy the following profiles of the stars...

Daisy Smears

Daisy Smears was discovered performing at a popular amusement park at age 14. Since then she has starred in movies such as *My Life at the Mall, Only One Pair of Shoes—The Horror Movie, Manners are Mud,* and a few more she would rather not discuss. She has been a guest star on the reality show *No Brainer*, and is a member of the Animals Are More Than People club. Her newest Daisy Doll is to be released next year, pending the patent on Plastic Surgery Daisy. Her authorized biography: *Math is Hard and Other Lessons I Learned as a Hollywood Expert* is a standard textbook for English class in Liberaland public schools. Daisy looks forward to one day completing junior high.

Rayonna

Rayonna was discovered as a child star, playing Candy on the TV sitcom, Bratty Bunch. Following the series, she reached number one with her hit single "I Don't Like Anything (Especially You)." The title track to her platinum CD "Caffeine" has earned her a Grammy. "Toenails, Turnips and Intuition," a ballad with legendary folk singer Bob Grunion, also climbed to the top spot on the charts. Rayonna is on the Board of Directors for the Save the Cauliflower National Monument Fund and is Grand Manicurian (CA Sect) of People Who Profess Toenailology. Next year she plans to change her name to ToeJamma. Rayonna has just released a cookbook, *101 Turnip Salad Recipes of the Stars,* and her do-it-yourself body piercing and tattooing kits are available exclusively at Back Alley Boutiques.

Congresswoman Clunkton

Congresswoman Clunkton has long been a star in the Liberaland Socialist Party (LSP). She has spent years riding the coattails of her husband, former President William Jefferson Clunkton, who is not often at home. Although Ms. Clunkton has introduced the Anti-sugar-in-your-lemonade Law, she's done little else for fear of losing her reputation of being a "moderate." Clunkton has decided that she needs to run for President, because, in her own mind, she's special and wants to "give back" to the Liberaland community; tax refunds, local control over schools and certain campaign contributions obtained at Hollywood galas are not among the items she's planning to return.

Barbara Buttersand

Barbara is the daughter of legendary actor/businessman Ben Acorn. She has starred in movies since the age of five. Her recent movies include: "Tales of a Secret Politician" and "Queenie," which earned her an Oscar and included the number one soundtrack and hit song "Elitist." Her album "It's All About Me," hit platinum in 2004. Currently President of the Actors Guild of Liberaland, she served as Special Ambassador to the White House for eight years. Her autobiography, *I'm Special, You're Not*, has topped the Liberaland Bestseller list for 40 weeks. Butter Boots and Barbara's signature radish earrings are available only in Beverly Hills and select presidential libraries. Barbara is currently married to her fifth husband, Jorgen Young, and serves as an unpaid advisor to the Clunkton for President Campaign.